Charles Holmes Herty

The Double Halides of Lead and the Alkali Metals

Charles Holmes Herty

The Double Halides of Lead and the Alkali Metals

ISBN/EAN: 9783337380311

Printed in Europe, USA, Canada, Australia, Japan

Cover: Foto ©Andreas Hilbeck / pixelio.de

More available books at **www.hansebooks.com**

The Double Halides

of

Lead and the Alkalies

A Dissertation

presented to the Board of University Studies of the
Johns Hopkins University for the Degree
of Doctor of Philosophy.

By

Chas. H. Herty.

1890

Acknowledgments

The author of this dissertation desires to express his most sincere thanks to Professor Ira Remsen at whose suggestion the work was undertaken and with whose constant advice it has been conducted.

The author desires to express his thanks also to Doctors Morse and Renouf for valuable instruction, and finally to Doctors Williams and Clark under whom the course in Mineralogy and Geology was pursued.

Table of Contents

[illegible]

in the time a very sharp distinction was drawn between the oxygen acids and bases. But now this sharp distinction no longer holds good, for many substances act either as acid or base, according to the nature of the substance with which it combines, thus Aluminium Hydroxide when treated with strong acids acts as a base, giving rise to aluminium salts of the acids, but when treated with ~~potassium hydrox~~ strong bases it acts as an acid, giving rise to a class of compounds called aluminates. In fact the oxygen compounds form a

aluminous series in which beginning with the strongest bases, the basic properties gradually diminish while the acid properties increase.

Just as the acidic oxides combine with the basic oxides to form salts, so, according to Von Bonsdorff,[1] stated acidic halides combine with basic halides to form compounds analogous to the salts.

In the same year, 1826, Boullay[2] called attention to the similarity between the oxides, halides, & sulphides, & put forward the idea that just as oxygen acids & bases combine to form

(1) Ann. Chim. phys. (2), 34, 142

(2) Ann. chim. phys. (2), 34, 337

oxygen salts or haloides combine with each other to form true salts; similarly sulphides combine with each other to form sulpho salts. Dr. [illegible] Vase of Philadelphia in his Compendium recognized the close analogy between the oxy, Sulpho, Chloro, Bromo and Iodo salts.

But these views of [illegible] Bonsdorff, Boullay and Vase were not generally accepted; the majority of Chemists rested satisfied with considering these bodies molecular compounds and not true Chemical compounds. In accordance with this idea they express the composition of these bodies in the following manner

F

Professor Remsen of Johns Hopkins University in an extended article on the "Nature and Structure of the Double Halides" has shown that from an examination of the composition of this large class of compounds the following law may be deduced.
"When a halide of any element combines with a halide of an alkali metal to form a double salt the number of molecules of the [deleted] alkali salt which are added to one molecule of the other halide is never greater

[illegible] 11 0 2 11

is never less than the number of halogen atoms contained in the latter."

In view of the facts embraced under this law, and the above analogy between the act involved in the formation of the double halides and that of the oxygen salts, and further the similarity between the products so formed, he offers the following explanation for these compounds:-

"Two halogen atoms are playing the same part that the so-called linking oxygen atoms play in oxygen salts."

This view has been held by some chemists, in more or less modified form, for some time,

Magnet(1) in 186[illegible] was the first to apply this explanation. He explained the compound of Silver Chloride and Potassium Chloride in the formula

$$\begin{matrix}Ag\\K\end{matrix} > Cl_2$$

in which the Chlorine is bivalent.

Blomstrand(2) in 1869 [illegible] some what similar formula for the double Chloride of Magnesium and Potassium, thus:-

$$Mg \begin{matrix}Cl\\Cl\end{matrix} Cl\,K$$

the chlorine here also is a bivalent element.

---

(1) Principes [illegible] sur les theories [illegible].

(2) Die Chemie der Jetztzeit vom Standpunkte der electro-chemischen Auffassung aus Berzelius Lehre entwickelt.

If we assume it acceptable that the halogen atoms can play the same part in the linking as oxygen does, then a remarkably close analogy is seen to exist between the oxygen acids and the double halides. Thus

$$Al\begin{cases}(Cl_2)Na\\(Cl_2)Na\\(Cl_2)Na\end{cases} \longleftrightarrow Al\begin{cases}ONa\\ONa\\ONa\end{cases}$$

Again

$$Si\begin{cases}F\\F\\(F_2)K\\(F_2)K\end{cases} \longleftrightarrow Si\begin{cases}O\\OK\\OK\end{cases}$$

The principal objection against this view is that emphasized by Professor Werner,* namely, that the halogen atoms must be considered not as bivalent elements, [illegible].

* Neuere Anschauungen auf dem Gebiete der anorganischen Chemie.

reaction was any stand in view of the existence of such compounds as KCl_3, KI_3 &c. these further the exceptions have been shown to be the equivalent towards oxygen. Therefore it is difficult to see why this objection should be urged any longer.

In reading the article in Graham Otto's Lehrbuch der "inorganischen Chemie" on the combinations of the iodide with potassium iodide we cannot fail to be struck with the fact that the different combinations of these bodies forms a well marked exception to the law of combination (without a change) of alkali halides with other halides.

~~Combination~~ For in addition to

[illegible]

$PbI_2 \cdot KI$ and

[illegible] I_2 [illegible]

here were mentioned also the compounds

$3PbI_2 \cdot 4KI$

$PbI_2 \cdot 4KI$ and

$PbI_2 \cdot 5KI$

On account of these results this investigation was undertaken to determine whether the combinations of Lead Iodide with Potassium Iodide really formed an exception to the above laws. In order to do this all the work previously done on this subject was carefully repeated & the conditions of the several experiments varied in every way possible.

The investigation was then extended

to the corresponding chlorine and Bromine Compounds, with regard to which very little was known.

It was hoped that the work could be extended to the Fluorine Compounds and to mixed Compounds containing more than one halogen, but this could not be accomplished on account of lack of time. It is hoped that in the future the portion of the investigation can be completed.

Method of Analysis

It may be noted that in giving the results of their work on the double iodides of lead and potassium neither Berthelot nor Ditte give the methods used by them for the analyses of the salts, although results are given by each for complete analyses. It is difficult to decide just what conclusion to draw from this fact. To say the least of it, when we look at it in the most charitable light one cannot be led to suppose that the analyses of the salts must be such a simple matter that it does not deserve to be

[illegible] [illegible], [illegible], [illegible]
for from the [illegible] [illegible]
working on the subject for
ten years [illegible] [illegible] the conclusion
that no absolutely trustworthy method
for complete analysis has yet
been found. [illegible] composition
of most of the salts prepared in
his investigation was deduced
from the determinations of
water of crystallization and
Lead. The water was
determined by heating to 110° a
weighed quantity of the salt
dried by pressing carefully
between drying paper.

In another portion the Lead was
determined thus;—
A weighed portion of the salt was [illegible]

introduced into an Erlenmeyer flask of 125 cc. capacity. Enough concentrated sulphuric acid to decompose the salt was then poured on it. The flask was then inclined to prevent loss by spattering and a very gentle heat was applied, until all the Iodine had been given off, the Lead and Potassium being now in the form of sulphates.

Close examination of the flask was showed that small & clean particles of Lead Iodide remained undecomposed on the sides of the flask. This was then washed down with concentrated sulphuric acid, and the mass was then thoroughly boiled for about

in sand bath in order to insure
the conversion of all Lead Iodide
into sulphate. After cooling
the mass was diluted to about
100 cc. & a small quantity
of alcohol added so that
any Lead sulphate being dissolved
allowed to stand then until the
supernatant liquid was
perfectly clear. Then
filtered into a Gooch crucible,
the $PbSO_4$ was then washed
thoroughly first with water to
which a little sulphuric acid
and alcohol had been added
in order to remove all traces
of Potassium sulphate then
washed with water containing a
little alcohol in order to remove

of sulphuric acid. The mixture was then dried thoroughly at 110° & finally heated to a very low red heat. Then allowed to cool twenty minutes in a dessicator and weighed.

To determine the Potassium by simple evaporation of the filtrate containing Potassium Sulphate & Sulphuric Acid is not practicable on account of the large excess of sulphuric acid necessarily present.

Experiments were made on the separation of Lead as Sulphide by Hydrogen Sulphide, but it was found that in every case some of the Lead sulphide remained in

solution cannot be made owing to the presence of the silicic acid. Various other methods were tried, all of which proved of no value.

The method finally adopted was as follows:-

1. One portion of the salt, water of crystallization was determined by heating to [illegible]° in an air bath.
2. The second portion, soda was determined by conversion into the sulphate, as described above.
3. One third portion, sodium and Potassium were determined thus. About one gramme of the salt was heated with 100 cc. water in a [illegible] beaker. This was stirred thoroughly

in order to prevent [illegible] the decomposition of [illegible] [illegible] then filtered into a Gooch crucible <u>without</u> <u>washing</u>, for if water [is] added to the filtrate Lead Iodide separates.

The Iodine in the filtrate was then precipitated as AgI

The residue in the Gooch crucible was then washed with cold water & the washings again passed through the crucible in order to retain any Lead Iodide which may have separated and to insure all Potassium Iodide being removed from the crucible.

This second filtrate is never added to the first in which the [illegible] is already

excess of Silver Nitrate
The Silver Iodide was then dried and
weighed. The Lead Iodide
in the crucible was then dried
& weighed. From the combined
amounts of Lead Iodide and Silver
Iodide the total amount of
Iodine was calculated.
4 The filtrate from the Silver
Iodide was then treated with Hydrogen
Sulphide, in order to remove
all Lead and Silver, filtered and evaporated
to dryness with Sulphuric acid
The residue of Potassium Sulphate
was heated to redness and weighed
from which the amount of
Potassium was calculated.
Analysed in this way the crystalline
salt obtained on dissolving

and iodine in a hot solution of Potassium Iodide, (saturated at 22°) on cleaning in cool gave the following results:

1. Determination of Water of crystallization

Weight of salt used 2.0016 grms

" water lost .083

Percentage of water [illegible]

2. Determination of Lead

Weight of salt used [illegible] grm

Lead sulphate formed .3687

Lead present .2518

Percentage of Lead = 30.84 %

3. Determination of Iodine.

Weight of salt used [illegible]41 grms

Lead Iodide .1137 "

Iodine in Lead Iodide .[illegible]157

Silver Iodide .220

Iodine in Silver Iodide .3361

[illegible] of [illegible] 3.[illegible]0 [illegible]

Percentage of Iodine 57.[illegible]1 %

Determination of Potassium

Weight of [illegible] used [illegible] 1

Potassium Sulphate 2 [illegible]

Potassium [illegible] 1 6

Percentage of Potassium 6.23 %

Summary

	Found	Calculated
Water	5.47 %	5.[illegible]3 %
Lead	30.[illegible] %	31.23 %
Iodine	57.31 %	57.[illegible]3 %
Potassium	6.23 %	5.71 %
Total	99.43 %	100.00 %

This composition was calculated for the salt $PbI_2 . KI . 2H_2O$ or as it should more correctly be written $KPbI_3 . 2H_2O$.

This analysis proved that [illegible]

n then for determination of [illegible] of
crystallization and lead was
corrected before [illegible] salts
were identified and their composition deduced from the determinations of water and lead.
In all the calculations the atomic weights given by Meyer and Seubert were used.

The amount of lead present in a given amount of lead sulphate was determined in all the analyses by multiplying the weight of lead sulphate by the factor 0.683

Potassium Iodo Plumbite.

(Salt of the Composition)

I. ($KPbI_3 . 2H_2O$ or ($PbI_2 . KI . 2H_2O$).–

The first work on the subject of the combinations of Lead Iodide with Potassium Iodide was done by Boullay[1] who in 27 announced as the result of his work the existence of the two salts $PbI_2 . KI$ and $PbI_2 . 4KI$.

The last named salt forms a very marked exception to the laws of combination of the alkali halides with other halides. As the work of Boullay has been carried out quite a long time ago I was (?) advisable [illegible]

[1] Ann. de Chim. Phys. 2 - 34 - [illegible]

[illegible]

determinations were not so accurate as they might have been, and furthermore the filter pump was not then in common use so that the methods for preparation of the salts must have been rather crude.

The first reports were [illegible] relate to the preparation of the salt $PbI_2 \cdot KI$ described by Boullay. The potassium Iodide used in these experiments was purified by recrystallizing. Iodate present by Zinc amalgam. The lead first used was prepared by precipitating lead Nitrate solution

---

[illegible] Boston, Amer. [illegible] 10 — 321

[illegible]
the latter portion of the investigation commercial Lead Iodide prepared by H. L. Thomson and Co. of Baltimore was used and the results agreeing very well with those obtained by using the Lead Iodide specially prepared.

According to Barclay, when Lead Nitrate is added to a slightly concentrated solution of Potassium Iodide there is formed first a red precipitate of Lead Iodide, which soon turns white owing to the conversion of the Lead Iodide into the double salt $PbI_2 . KI$ by the Potassium Iodide present in the solution. Great trouble was experienced

it was [illegible] on boiling its salt.
As Barclay [illegible] a use a
solution of Potassium Iodide
only slightly concentrated.
In each of the preliminary experiments
Lead Iodide was precipitated when
Lead Nitrate solution was added
to a solution of Potassium
Iodide only slightly concentrated,
But on standing, whether
cold or hot, there was no
change to a white colour as
described by Barclay; the
Lead Iodide remaining unchanged
in the solution. But when
a solution of Potassium Iodide
a little more concentrated was
used and heat applied it was
noticed that yellow needles form

ing the evaporation of the beaker in which the experiment was being conducted, where drops of the solution had spattered, the drops becoming more concentrated by evaporation.

This suggested that if a more concentrated solution of Potassium Iodide were used, the salt might be obtained. Experiments were then made to determine the exact conditions under which the salt is formed.

To this effect a solution of Lead Nitrate was made up so that 1 c.c. = 0.25 gramme. Further a Potassium Iodide solution of such a strength that 1 c.c. = 0.25 gramme.

Five portions of the Lead Nitrate

amount of five cubic centimeters each were then measured out.

To these were added quantities of the Potassium Iodide solution (normal) varying from 5 c.c. to 25 c.c. Lead Iodide was precipitated in each case but on cooling the mass did not turn white as described by Barclay in any of the five portions.

So to five portions were (5 c.c. (norm) of the Potassium Iodide solution were added successively quantities of [illegible] solid Potassium Iodide varying from 0.25 grm. to 1.25 grm. These solutions were heated & added to the five portions (5 c.c. norm) of the Lead Nitrate solution

[illegible] was precipi-
tated in each case [illegible] still there
was no double salt formed.
So again to five portions of 5 c.c. each
of the potassium iodide solution were added [illegible]
potassium iodide varying from
3.0 grms to 5.0 grms. The solutions
were then heated and added to
five portions 5 c.c. each of Lead
Nitrate solution. [illegible] iodide
was precipitated in each case
[illegible] gradually the red precipitate
becomes white the most concentrated solution becoming white first.
On heating these masses the
white salt is decomposed [illegible]
and insoluble Lead Iodide remains
having the form of the original
crystals but [illegible] [illegible] [illegible]

[illegible] became white, owing to the formation of the insoluble salt as described by Barclay. This slightly yellowish salt was freed from the mother liquor as much as possible by means of a filter pump, then pressed between drying paper, then placed in a dessicator for twelve hours. The following results were obtained by analysis.

1. Determination of water of crystallization

weight of salt used = [illegible] grms

water lost [illegible]

percentage of water = [illegible].14 %

2. Determination of Lead

weight of salt used = 1.613[illegible] grms

Lead Sulphate [illegible].[illegible][illegible]23

Lead [illegible].4717

Percentage of lead 21.1

Determination of water of crystallization after standing over sulphuric acid one week

weight of salt used = 1.02 grams

after test - 1.28

Percentage of water 0.27 %

Summary

	Found 1%	2%	Calculated for Pb... I (Brandling)
Water	1.14%	0.273%	—
Lead	29.70%	—	33.02

... this salt lost its water of crystallization by standing over sulphuric acid a dehydrating agent and therefore showed not to be based in this way

... the mother liquor of this salt upon standing ... after standing formed long needles of slightly yellowish color ... Pb ...

elevation [illegible] [illegible] [illegible]
[illegible] redissolved in the mother
liquor [illegible] rapidly heating
the beaker [illegible] with
a free flame [illegible] [illegible]
accompanied [illegible] remaining
[illegible] which retains the [illegible] of
the original crystals. On cooling
these needles again became white.

The explanation of the formation of these long needles in the mother liquor will be given under the head of the salt
$3\,PtI_2 . 4\,AsI_3 . [illegible]$.

The salt $PtI_2 . AsI_3$ [illegible] was then prepared in larger quantities by using the following proportions
[illegible]

[illegible] water [illegible]

[illegible] in [illegible] crystals in solution

was then heated [illegible] the

sand nitrate solution cooled rapidly,

stirring all the while.

The double salt thus formed was

pumped dry & pressed between

drying paper for twenty four

hours.

This salt [illegible] gave the

following results.

[illegible] Estimation of water by crystallization

a) – weight of double salt used 3.6[illegible] grms

water lost 1.[illegible]2 "

Percentage of water [illegible].22%

b) – weight of salt used [illegible] grms

water lost – [illegible]

Percentage of water – [illegible].25 %

2 [illegible] of Lead

a) Weight of salt used [illegible] 1 [illegible]

Lead Sulphate 0.[illegible] 2

Lead [illegible].3301

Percentage of Lead 30.[illegible] %

b) weight of salt used .36[illegible] grms

Lead Sulphate [illegible] 1 [illegible] 2

Lead [illegible] 201

Percentage of Lead = 30.06 %

c) weight of salt used [illegible].88[illegible] grms

" Lead Sulphate [illegible] 02 "

" Lead = [illegible].2733

Percentage of Lead 30.82 %

Summary

Found	Calculated for $PbX_2 . K_2 . 2H_2O$
1st - 2nd - 3rd	
Water - 5.22 - 5.25	5.43
Lead - 30.[illegible] 30.[illegible] 30.82	31.23

From these figures the composition

of the salt in iodine is
KPbI3. 2 H2O or PbI2 KI. 2 H2O
Boullay prepared this salt
but dried it over lime.
Accordingly he found only 3.4
of water; says " Si l'on
suppose que l'eau de sel
ou deux iodures soient à
l'état d'hydriodates il
faudrait 4.14 d'eau pour
100 parties du sel humide;
je n'en ai trouvé que 3.00"
In speaking of the formation of
this salt Boullay states that
it is always formed when a
slightly concentrated solution
of potassium iodide is brought
together, but on cold such an

Ann. Chim. Phys. 2, 34, 367

excess of [illegible] cyanide. It is difficult to understand why he should have made this statement as his evidence [illegible] his remark on the subject [illegible] he never worked with an excess of Lead Iodide but that in each case the Iodide was first precipitated & this was then converted into the double salt or Iodoplumbite by the excess of KI in the solution.

[illegible] in order to test his statement strictly [illegible] a solution of Potassium Iodide not quite saturated at 20° was added to a large excess of Lead [illegible] Iodide in a beaker

measured promptly. It was on cooling the excess of Lead Iodide collected at the bottom while the supernatant liquid remained clear. But on the following day silky needle shaped crystals were found in the solution & also mixed with pure Lead Iodide in the bottom. The crystals were removed from the solution dried and analysed giving the following results.

1. Determination of Lead.

weight of salt used	0.2175 g
Lead Sulphate	[illegible]
Lead	.1054
Percentage of Lead	[illegible].121
Theoretical for $KPbI_3 \cdot 2H_2O$	31.231

This was repeated in the same [illegible]

fact is seen and is because

Some of the needle shaped crystals of the salt $\cdot SO_3 \cdot 2H_2O$ were then heated to [illegible] latest which very more water could be driven off but no greater loss was found than by heating to 10[illegible] so hence [illegible] molecules of water of crystallization present in the salt.

The further effect of heat upon this salt was seen in this way. Some of the needle shaped crystals were placed in an ignition tube this in turn was placed in [illegible] tube in sulphuric acid bath. The temperature raised gradually. [illegible] water began to come off the salt [illegible]

weighted we have a corresponding
considerably in bulk. The
temperature was raised the amount
of water given off increased to
such an extent that it collected
in drops on the sides
of the tube. These drops
falling on the salt placed
recombined it instantly as
was shown by the colour of
the hydrate which
appeared. Thus the same
water which had been present
in the compound as water
of crystallization after having
been driven out by heat
served to recombine the anhydrous
salt when brought in contact
with it. [illegible]

ignition tube heat at an angle in order to prevent the water falling back upon the salt it was shown that at about 310° the salt decomposed iodine being given off.

Treated with absolute alcohol this salt is decomposed just as when treated with water.

It is not possible to determine the concentration at which the salt $KPbI_3 . 2H_2O$ was formed, as mentioned above. Attempts were then made to prepare the salt $PbI_2 . 4KI$ described by Barclay(1) under the head of Bibasic Iodoplumbate of Iodide of Potassium, both made by adding Lead Iodide to a concentrated solution of Potassium Iodide, this last being in excess. He represented the composition of the salt by the formula $2KaI_4 + PbI_2$ or according to the present names as $PbI_2 + KI$.

(1) Ann. Ch. Phys. [2] 34 370

The formula was based upon the following analyses.

	Found 1st analysis	Found 2nd analysis	Calculated for $PbI_2 + 4KI$
Lead Iodide	34.0	36.0	41.0 %
Potassium Iodide	66.0	64.0	59.0 %

Efforts were now directed to repeating his work, in order to see whether the salt really existed, for if it exists it forms a very striking exception to the law of combination of the [illegible] halides with other halides mentioned in the introduction.

A cold saturated solution of Potassium Iodide Lead Nitrate was added [illegible]

white scales was obtained
It was the first crystallization of
Lead & Potassium Iodides
obtained in this investigation,
It was dried not by pumping
off the mother liquor but by
simple filtration [illegible]
between drying paper for a
short while & finally completely
dried by standing over
Lime, the method adopted
by Barclay,
This salt gave on analysis
the following results

Determinations of water of crystallization

a) weight of salt used - 1.2961 grms

" water lost 0.0388 "

Percentage of water 2.99 %

b) weight of salt used = .27[illegible] grms

" water lost - .0[illegible]1 "

Percentage of water 1.50 %

2. - Determinations of Lead

a) weight salt used 0.3880 grms.

" of Lead Sulphate = 0.14351 "

" Lead - 0.0980 "

Percentage of Lead - 25.26 %

b) weight salt used 2.3640 grms

" Lead Sulphate 0.9015 "

" Lead .6157

Percentage of Lead = 26.04

	Summary of Found (in case of analysis)		Calculated for $PbI_2 : 4KI$
Water of Crystallization	2.71	1.50	
Lead	25.26	26.04	[illegible]

These results show that [illegible] the salt [illegible] sought has not been obtained but rather a salt approaching in composition the salt $PbI_2 . 2$ [illegible] $. 4H_2O$ described by Ditte[1] with the exception of the water, which is shown by the difference in the two analyses, the second having been made several days after the first, that water was abstracted by the lime over which the salt stood.

The preparation of this salt and its analyses were rather crude as they were the first attempts; however the results were sufficient to

---

Ann. Ch. Ph. [5] 21 226

shown that the salt Ca_2 was had not been formed under the conditions named.

Later in the investigation another attempt was made to prepare this salt following the directions of Barclay, but the salt instead of being dried over lime was pressed for several days between drying paper & carefully analysed.

The following results were obtained

1. Determination of water of crystallization

a) weight of salt was 1.2106 grm

water lost 0.0634

percentage of water = 5.24 %

b) weight of salt used 0.137
water lost [illegible]
Percentage of water - 5.23 %

2. Determinations of Lead

a) weight of salt used [illegible] gms
Lead Sulphate = 0.[illegible]561
" Lead 0.3121 "
Percentage of Lead - 30.75 %

b) weight of salt used [illegible].8693 gms.
Lead Sulphate = 0.39[illegible] "
" Lead 0.2673
Percentage of Lead = 30.75

Summary

	Found		Calculated
	Analyses [illegible]		[illegible]
Water	5.2[illegible]	5.23	—
Lead	30.75	30.75	18.40

Chemical Composition of [illegible] [illegible] $2H_2$

[illegible] water = 5.23 Lead = 3[illegible] 23

i salt therefore in obtaining the salt [illegible] . [illegible] 2 [illegible] [illegible] [illegible] $PbI_3.2H_2O$.

The results differed very widely from those first obtained in trying to prepare the salt $PbI_2.HI$. In the first case the percentage of lead was 25.20%; in the second case 30.10%. Many efforts were then made to obtain the salt which yielded 25.20% of lead by varying the conditions [illegible] in all possible ways, but in no case was anything obtained even approaching this composition, therefore it seems justifiable to conclude that the salt [illegible]

25.2 salt was prepared & analysed in a rather rough way must have been very impure owing to excess of Potassium Iodide present.

From the above facts it is to be concluded that the salt $PbI_2.KI$ does not exist & that it probably consisted of the salt $PbI_3.2H_2O$ mixed with quite a large amount of Potassium Iodide.

A salt of this composition is
mentioned in Graham-Otto
Lehrbuch der Anorganischen
Chemie" and is ascribed to Barclay,
but no reference is given to
the article in which Barclay
describes this salt.
All the articles of Barclay on
this subject were then
carefully examined, but no
such salt could be found.
In searching through the Jahresbericht
of Berzelius & the Jahresbericht
now published, no account of
this salt can be found.
But in order to make the
proof of its non existence

still more besides all the journals in the Chemical Library of the Johns Hopkins University were examined.

This work consumed about **two** months time and a record no trace of the salt $PbI_2.2KI$ could be found.

Further in all the experiments on the combinations of Lead Iodide with Potassium Iodide there was at no time found a salt whose composition approached in any degree the formula $PbI_2.2KI$.

Therefore it is almost probable that this is an error in the "Lehrbuch der Anorganischen Chemie".

———

IV. Salts of the Composition, $K_2PbI_4.4H_2O$ ($PbI_2.2KI.4H_2O$)[1] and $K_2PbI_4.2H_2O$ (or $PbI_2.2KI.2H_2O$). (Ditte)

Since the paper published by Boullay in 1827 the principal work on the double Iodides of Lead & Potassium has been done by Ditte & also by Berthelot.

Ditte[1] described the salt $PbI_2.2KI.4H_2O$ giving on account of its [illegible] of [illegible] appearance general behavior & studied its decomposition by water.

Berthelot[2] then took up the subject and described the two

---

(1) Ann. Ch. Phys. [5] 24 226

(2) Ann. Ch. Phys. [5] 29 201

salt [illegible] is

KI_2 [illegible] $KI . 6H_2O$

The investigation was then turned to the repetition of the work of these Chemists. Both agree that the salts ($PbI_2 . 2KI . 4H_2O$) and ($PbI_2 . 2KI . 2H_2O$) are formed.

Both agree that the salt containing Lead & Potassium Iodides in the proportion of one part of Lead Iodide to two of Potassium Iodide is formed whenever Lead Iodide is added to a warm solution of Potassium Iodide & the solution allowed to cool. Ditte also states that the salt is formed in the cold.

[illegible] previously stated when [illegible]

recently been first
begun a salt was obtained
which seemed to have the
composition $PtI_2 \cdot 2KI$.
The water of crystallization not
being constant.

But now on the first attempt
to repeat the work of Nitte,
a salt was obtained resembling
in appearance that described by
Nitte and which on analysis
gave the following results—

1. Determination of water of crystallization

weight of salt used	2227	grms
" water lost	0 3	"
Percentage of water	3.38 %	

2 determinations of Lead

(1) weight of salt used 2.1521 grm

Lead Sulphate .9541

Lead .6517 "

Percentage of Lead = 30.28 %

(2) weight of salt used .7733 grm

Lead Sulphate [illegible]

Lead .2334

Percentage of Lead 30.14 %

Summary

	Found analysis 1	2 analysis	Calculated for $PbI_2.2KI.2H_2O$
Water	3.38	—	5.33 %
Lead	30.28	30.14	31.37 %

This composition agrees more closely with the salt $KPbI_3.2H_2O$ for which the water = 5.43 % and Lead 31.23 %. A water of crystallization [illegible] because the salt was partially dried [illegible]

a salt (as mentioned) was prepared from a hot solution.
As it had been shown earlier that heat decomposes the salt $PbI_2.KI.2H_2O$ Lead Iodide separating from the mass, it was thought probable that the salt $PbI_2.2KI.4H_2O$ would be formed in the cold.
To this end 50 c.c. of a cold saturated solution of Potassium Iodide was added to 10 c.c. of a cold saturated solution of Lead Nitrate.
The Lead Iodide precipitated soon turned white owing to the formation of the double salt.
As the mass became pasty more of the Potassium Iodide solution was added, enough to render the mass quite mobile, to ensure

[illegible] decanted into the crucible & salt.

The salt prepared in this way was analysed by boiling with Sodium Carbonate the Lead being thus changed to Carbonate & then into a Gooch Crucible washed thoroughly & ignited at a low red heat. The Lead was then weighed as Lead Oxide. The following results were obtained.

Determinations of water of crystallization

1) weight of salt used = .7823 gms.

water lost = 0.0766 "

Percentage of water = 5.427%

2) weight of salt used = .653 gms

water lost .0892

Percentage of water 5.37%

2. Determination of Lead

Weight of salt used = 2[illegible] gms

Lead oxide 0.[illegible]170

Lead [illegible]

Percentage of Lead 31.20 %

Summary

	1st analysis	2nd analysis	Calculated for $KPI_3 \cdot 2H_2O$
Water	5.42	5.37	5.43 %
Lead	31.20	(not calculated)	3[illegible]23 %

In this method, after preparing the salt $KPI_2 \cdot 2H_2O$ either had failed it was then attempted to prepare the salt by heating a cold saturated solution of Potassium Iodide almost to boiling then adding Lead Iodide to saturation but this was found impracticable since such large quantities of Lead Iodide are taken

up in solution but no double
salt seems to separate from the
solution at the surface while
Lead Iodide is still being
taken up. So to a hot solution
of Potassium Iodide (cold saturated)
Lead Iodide was added in quite
large quantity but not enough
to cause the separation of
the salt as mentioned above.
On cooling pale yellow needle
shaped crystals separated.
These were dried & marked "1".
The filtrate from this salt was
moderately diluted with water
& some bright coloured crystals
were seen to appear. On standing
a short while the whole mass became
almost solid owing to the thick

in mass of needles shape crystals formed. These were dried & marked #2. — By continuing the dilution crystals began to appear again but now on adding more water these crystals were decomposed into Lead Iodide & Potassium Iodide however on stirring the mass thoroughly the original white color was restored. These crystals were dried & marked #3. By further dilution of the filtrate still a fourth crop of crystals was obtained. These were marked #4. But now on adding ~~more~~ water & a small portion of the filtrate decomposition took place immediately Lead Iodide separating in large quantities.

~~By further dilution [illegible]~~
~~[illegible] which were dried & marked #4.~~

But on heating water because of the filtrate with alcohol a flocculent white salt separated which on close examination seemed to be composed of little needles.
These were marked #5.
It was thought that the five specimens would form to be a series of compounds showing a gradation in composition.
The following results were obtained from the analyses.

1. Determinations of water of crystallization

#1) weight of salt used — .63 × mm
water lost .013
Percentage of water 2.5 %

#2) weight of salt used .2032 mm
water lost .0117
Percentage of water 5.13 %.

#3) weight of salt used .2[illegible] gms
water lost - [illegible]613 "
Percentage of water .271
[illegible] weight of salt used 1.1226 gms
water lost - .0591
Percentage of water = 5.26 %
#5) weight of salt used 1.2413 gms
" " water lost = 0.0637
Percentage of water = 5.15 %
2nd determinations of Lead
#1) weight of salt used = 1.6216 gms
" " Lead Sulphate - 0.7300
Lead = 0.4986
Percentage of Lead = 30.75 %
#2) weight of salt used = 1.1969 gms
" Lead Sulphate = 0.5371
Lead = 0.3682
Percentage of Lead = 30.76 %

#3) weight of salt used [illegible].278[illegible] gms.

Lead Sulphate [illegible].5[illegible]02 "

Lead [illegible]3[illegible]1

Percentage of Lead [illegible]0.10 %

#4) weight of salt used 1.1226 gms

" Lead Sulphate = 0.5046 "

" " Lead = 0.34[illegible]81 "

Percentage of Lead = 31.01 %

#5) weight of salt used 1.2[illegible] 3 gms

" Lead Sulphate = [illegible].5637 "

" Lead = [illegible].3850

Percentage of Lead = 31.[illegible]2 %

Summary

	Found #1	#2	#3	#4	#5	Calculated for $KPbI_3 . 2H_2O$
Water	5.28	5.13	5.17	5.26	5.15	5.43 %
Lead	30.75	30.76	30.90	31.01	31.02	31.23 %

The [illegible] as seen in almost all of the analyses below the theoretical. This is to be expected as the mother liquor [illegible]

is rich in Potassium Iodide cannot be washed out but has to be pressed out. This would therefore cause the results on water & lead to fall below the theoretical.

An examination of the above table shows that instead of obtaining a series of salts, the same salt had been obtained in each case, becoming gradually poorer as the solution was diluted. Barclay observed this same phenomenon.

These facts also show that the same salt $KPbI_3.2H_2O$ is obtained & not Ditte's salt $PbI_2.2KI.4H_2O$ whether a hot concentrated solution of Potassium Iodide is used or a cold solution increasing from considerable

concentration is just above the point where separation of Lead Iodide takes place, & still further dilution separates the same salt from this last most dilute solution.

This is very strong evidence against the existence of the salt $PbI_2 . 2KI . 4H_2O$ described by Ditte or $PbI_2 . 2KI . 2H_2O$ described by Berthelot.

Another solution was then prepared similar to that from which the salt marked #1 had been obtained, but, instead of filtering from the crystals formed, water was added. Lead iodide at first separated out, by stirring the mass thoroughly the original color was restored. This may

a large quantity of water was added until finally by further addition of water to a small portion of the mass Lead Iodide was seen to separate & remain so on stirring thoroughly. The analysis of the salt thus formed proved it to be the salt $KPbI_3 . 2H_2O$.

Efforts were then made to prepare the salt $PbI_2 . 2KI . 4H_2O$ by dissolving the salt $KPbI_3 . 2H_2O$ ($PbI_2 . KI . 2H_2O$) in a large excess of a cold saturated solution of Potassium Iodide heat being applied. The salt dissolved and on cooling long needle shaped crystals separated similar in appearance to the salt which had been dissolved. The following result was obtained by analysis

Determination of Lead

Weight of salt used	.07 4 grms
Lead Sulphate	.0442 "
Lead	1.3375 "
Percentage of Lead	30.75 %
Theoretical for $K'PbI_3.2H_2O$	31.23 %

All of these attempts to the preparation of the salt described by with Ditte & Berthelot having failed it was concluded to try once again following the directions of Ditte exactly. In this way a salt was obtained which when heated before separating from its mother liquor decomposed, the Lead Iodide so formed retaining the form of the original crystals. In filtering, water used [in] cleaning

On cooling a wet mass of needle shaped crystals was obtained which almost solidified the mass.

An analysis this salt gave the following results,

1st - Determination of water of crystallization

weight of salt used 1.2172 grms

" water lost .0650 "

Percentage of water - 5.34 %

2 Determination of Lead.

weight of salt used - .8407 grms

Lead Sulphate .3836 "

Lead .2620 "

Percentage of Lead 30.87 %

Summary

	Found	Calculated for $PbI_2.KI.2H_2O$	for $PbI_2.2KI.2H_2O$
Water	5.34 %	5.43	4.33 %
Lead	30.87 %	31.23 %	23.13 %

This was therefore the same salt

[illegible] has been obtained in all [illegible] previous experiments.

Mette[1] describes another method for the preparation of the salt $PbI_2 . 2KI . 4H_2O$ [illegible] as all previous efforts to prepare the salt had failed it was thought that by this means the salt might be obtained or on the other hand very conclusive evidence obtained that the salt does not exist.

This method of preparation consists in mixing freshly precipitated Lead Carbonate with an excess of a cold saturated solution of Potassium Iodide. [illegible] takes place at [illegible] and many impurities

---

[1] [illegible] Ch. Phy. [illegible] 2[illegible] 235

out unbroken a current of Carbon dioxide through the mixture for about twenty minutes, the white Lead Carbonate is replaced by the slightly yellowish crystals of the double salt. This salt gave by analysis the following results,

1. Determination of water of crystallization.

weight of salt used 0.7316 gms

" water lost = 0.0492 "

Percentage of water = [illegible] %

2. Determinations of Lead

a) weight of salt used [illegible]1653 gms

Lead Sulphate .4[illegible]

Lead .3392 "

Percentage of Lead 3[illegible]

b) weight of salt used [illegible]975 gms

Lead Sulphate [illegible]

Lead 0.2703 "

Percentage of Lead 3[illegible]

Summary

	Found 1st	2nd	Calculated for $PbI_2.2KI.2H_2O$
Water	5.28		5.4[illegible]
Lead	31.47	31.45	31.23

The salt $PbI_2.2KI.2H_2O$ described by Berthelot[1] was obtained, to use his own words "par le refroidissement de la solution de l'iodure de plomb dans une solution concentrée d'iodure de potassium."

Lately this condition has been tried repeatedly in the effort to prepare the salt $PbI_2.2KI$. [illegible] described by Ditte but in order to be absolutely certain that this salt of Berthelot's [illegible]

[1] Ann. Ch. Phys. [illegible] 287

until a balance, three successive attempts were made varying the conditions slightly in each case. The salts obtained in this way gave on analysis the following results.

1. Determination of water of crystallization

#1) weight of salt used .2175 gm
water lost .0565
Percentage of water [illegible].5[illegible] %

#2 weight of salt used .3076 gm
water lost .072[illegible] "
Percentage of water [illegible].22 %

#3) weight of salt used [illegible] gm
water lost [illegible]
Percentage of water [illegible].21 %

2 determinations of Lead

#1) weight of salt used [illegible]11 gms

Lead Sulphate [illegible]

Lead [illegible]

Percentage of Lead 30.[illegible] %

#2) weight of salt used [illegible]11 gms

" " Lead Sulphate = .2730 "

Lead [illegible] "

Percentage of Lead = 30.18 %

#3) weight of salt used [illegible] gms

Lead Sulphate .3567

Lead .2438 "

Percentage of Lead 30.30 %

Summary

	Found			Calculated for	
		2	3	$KPbI_3.2H_2O$	[illegible]$.2H_2O$
K	5.5	5.22	5.21	5.437	4.35 %
Lead	30.41	30.18	30.30	31.23 %	24.77 %

Showing that the salt has the composition $KPbI_3.2H_2O$.

solutions of Potassium Iodide saturated at or near their boiling with heat, were found to be of no value as when a rather small quantity of Lead Iodide was added, then on cooling a large mass of Potassium Iodide crystallized out along with the double salt; and when a large quantity of PbI_2 was added the mass soon became unmanageable on account of the large amount of double salt present in the solution, so that it could not be filtered or purified in any way.

From all of these facts it is to be concluded that the salts

cannot exist for not only have the directions of which Ditte & Berthelot been closely followed but ~~[illegible]~~ furthermore the conditions have been changed using at one time hot solutions at another cold, at one time cold saturated at another dilute again a solution of KI saturated at 100° was employed, & in each case the salt $KPbI_3, 2H_2O$ was obtained. ~~Further~~ I [illegible] attempted to make the salt by dissolving $KPbI_3, 2H_2O$ in a cold saturated solution of Potassium Iodide & finally by passing [illegible] dioxide through a mixture of Lead Carbonate

& Potassium iodide solution & here likewise was obtained the salt $KPbI_3 . 2H_2O$.

V. Salt of the Composition, $K_4Pb_3I_{10} \, 6H_2O$ $(3PbI_2 . 4KI . 6H_2O)$

This salt is described by Berthelot[1]. He in turn ascribes it to Boullay but gives no reference to an article by Boullay. Accordingly careful search was made for Boullay's description of this salt while looking for his account of the salt $PbI_2 . 5KI$ mentioned on page 49 but this search was unsuccessful.

Berthelot states that it is formed

---

[1] Ann. Ch. Phys. (5) 29 287

by slow cooling of the mother liquor from the salt [illegible] which in turn is prepared by adding Lead Iodide to a concentrated solution of Potassium Iodide. These directions were closely followed. The mother liquor from the salt which first separated on cooling being surrounded by water in order to lower the temperature was then allowed to stand four days. Long yellow needles separated which analysis showed the following results-

Determination of water of crystallization

Weight of salt used [illegible] grms.
water lost .382
Percentage of [illegible] 7.4

2. Determination of Lead

Weight of salt used = .1713 grm

" Lead Sulphate 1. 0 2 "

" Lead = 0.2740

Percentage of Lead 27.64 %

Summary

	Found	Calculated for $3PbI_2.4KI.6H_2O$	Calculated for $2PbI_2.3KI.4H_2O$
Water	4.87	5.02 %	4.83 %
Lead	27.64	28.82 %	27.75 %

This analysis seemed to show that the salt had the composition $2PbI_2.3KI.4H_2O$.

In order to confirm this the experiment was repeated, the mother liquor in this case being surrounded by ice. Long needles crystallized from the solution, but in addition considerable quantities of

Potassium Iodide also separated.
So the whole was heated gently
until all had passed into
solution. The beaker was then
placed on a desk in the Laboratory & allowed to cool.
The following night was very
cold and on examining the
beaker next morning there
could be seen that the double
salt & Potassium Iodide.
This was heated again until all dissolved,
& after several trials at different
temperatures finally a good
crop of beautiful long needles
was obtained which were
apparently free from Potassium
Iodide. This was analysed with
the following results -

Determination of water of Crystallization

weight of salt used 1.2121 gm

water lost 0.0647

Percentage of water = 5.33 %

2nd Determination of Lead.

weight of salt used = 0.6945

Lead Sulphate = 0.3140

" " Lead = 0.2145

Percentage of Lead = 30.88 %

Summary

	Found	Calculated for $K_2PbI_4 \cdot 2H_2O$
Water	5.33	5.43 %
Lead	30.88	31.23 %

These results showed that most probably in the first preparation of the salt, the temperature was reduced too low so that the salt was

mixed with potassium iodide In order to test this more fully Carefully the last experiment The work was very carefully repeated, accurate measurements being made at each stage, as follows:- 100 cc. of a solution of KI (sat. at 22°) was heated. When the temperature reached 75° cadmium iodide was added gradually while the temperature was being raised to 100°. In this way 17.5084 grms of iodide were added. The solution was then allowed to cool at 34 while shaken crystals began to separate. The cooling was continued until the temperature reached 22°. The mother liquor was

[illegible] [illegible] [illegible] [illegible] under
[illegible] [illegible] [illegible] when it was
allowed to remain for three
days the temperature varying
only slightly above or below
10°. Long needle shaped
crystals separated out [illegible]
and apparently free from
Potassium Iodide.
On analysis this salt gave
the following results:-

Determination of water of crystallization
Weight of salt used .1263 gms.
" water lost [illegible] "
Percentage of water - 2.12%

2. Determination of Lead
Weight of salt used - .2[illegible] gms
" Lead Sulphate = [illegible] "
" Lead .3787
Percentage of Lead - 30.56%

Summary

	Found	Calculated for $KPbI_3 . 2H_2O$	$3PbI_2 . 4KI . 6H_2O$
Water	5.12	5.43 %	5.02 %
Lead	30.56	31.23 %	28.82 %

From these facts it seems probable that the salt described by Berthelot as $3PbI_2 . 4KI . 6H_2O$ was really a mixture of the salts $KPbI_3 . 2H_2O$ and KI.

Indeed this is rendered more probable when it is remembered that at the temperature & concentration used, Potassium Iodide which is present in the solution in large excess, separates very easily as already shown.

on Sodium Iodo Bismuthite on

The literature in regard to this subject is extremely limited.

Barclay[1] states that it is probable that the other alkali Iodides would act like Potassium Iodide in regard to the formation of the double Iodide, but makes no experiments on the subject.

Nickles[2] dismisses the subject by stating that Sodium Iodide behaves like Potassium Iodide but gives no experimental data.

Jaggiale[3] mentions a double iodide of Lead & Sodium to which he ascribes the composition $PbI_2.NaI$ but the work

1 Amer. Ch. Jour. [2] 3[illegible] 372

2 Compt. Rend. 72 1[illegible]

3 Jour. Prakt. Chem. 35 3[illegible]

is not all reliable.

Efforts were even made to obtain this salt so that it could be analyzed & its composition determined. To this effect, 700 grms of Sodium Iodide were dissolved in 700 cc water at 20°. Lead Iodide was then added until no more dissolved, about 60 grms thereof was added.

This solution on standing gave back no crystals. The double salt in solution is therefore much more soluble than the corresponding potassium salt. The solution was then heated & 10 grms. more of Lead Iodide added. On cooling nothing crystallized out.

So the solution was then evaporated to about 2/3 of its former size.

on cooling needle shape crystals separated closely resembling the Potassium salt in appearance. These crystals formed in such large quantities that the mass almost completely solidified. Like the Potassium salt, this salt is decomposed by water & by heat with a separation of Lead Iodide. Great difficulty was experienced in purifying this salt, for such large quantities of Sodium Iodide were mixed with it. Various methods were tried for example, as Sodium Iodide is very deliquescent it was hoped that by allowing the mixture to stand exposed to moist air enough water would be taken up to dissolve

the sodium oxide & leave the soluble salt behind but this proved unavailable. The method finally adopted was as follows:-
The mixture was exposed to the air until quite a considerable quantity of water had been absorbed. The undissolved portion on being pressed with a stirring rod gave a gritty feel due to the sodium oxide present. Heat was then gently applied & it was soon found that the gritty feel had disappeared, only clear salt remaining in the solution. The heating was now discontinued & the mass filtered rapidly by means of filter pump (for if the heating is continued the metals passes into solution.)

the salt was then pressed between
drying paper for several days &
at the end of that time was found
to be still moist showing
that the salt itself was deliquescent,
& it was then dried in an [illegible] at
[illegible] the anhydrous salt,
which is a reddish-yellow
powder gave on analysis the following
results:-

<u>Determination of Lead:</u>

weight of salt used – [illegible] 1 gm

Lead Sulphate – .320

Lead = .2455

Percentage of Lead = 3[illegible].71 %

theoretical for $NaPbI_3$ – 33.89 %

The composition of the salt is
therefore very probably $NaPbI_3$,
nothing definite can be said as

[illegible] to the water of crystallization is the salt is so deliquescent that it can not be obtained dry at ordinary temperatures.

However it is very probable that the salt does contain water of crystallization ~~as no water~~ ~~form~~ its adding up to the potassium salt & from the fact that so much Sodium Iodide crystallizes out with the double salt the solution becoming very concentrated, probably on account of so much water being taken up by the ~~Pb~~ Sodium Iodides to form water of crystallization in the double salt.

Potassium Bromo Iodide

The only work hitherto on this subject up to the present time was that done by Berthelot(1). This was very unsatisfactory however & indeed he remarks that the substances obtained by him are not to be regarded as true Chemical Compounds but mixtures of the double salt with Potassium Bromide or Potass Br[illegible] &c. He gives however the composition of the salt obtained as

3PaIBr2. 2KIBr.

Efforts were now made to determine whether a definite compound

---

(1) Ann Ch Phys 5-21-2[illegible]

of Lead & Potassium Bromides could be obtained. It was found that if to a solution of Potassium Bromide saturated at 20° a solution of Lead Nitrate (saturated at 20°) is added, drop by drop, the Lead Bromide so formed will be dissolved on constant stirring until quite a large quantity has been dissolved though not nearly so large a quantity as in the case of the Iodides. When all the Lead Bromide possible had been dissolved the solution was allowed to stand and in about three hours colorless crystals began to form. After several days these tabular crystals grew to considerable size [illegible]. On analysis the following results were obtained, from the finely powdered and [illegible] salt.

Determinations of water of crystallization

(a) weight of salt used [illegible] 2 [illegible]

" water lost [illegible].0276 "

Percentage of water 3.[illegible]3 %

weight of salt used [illegible].15 12 gms

" water lost [illegible]

Percentage of water = 3.[illegible] %

2. Determinations of Lead

(a) weight of salt used 2.5[illegible]1 gms

Lead Sulphate .[illegible] "

Lead - .120

Percentage of Lead = [illegible] %

(b) weight of salt used = 2 [illegible] 1 gms

" Lead Sulphate [illegible]

" Lead = [illegible].30

Percentage of Lead [illegible].12 %

Summary

	Found			Calculated for [illegible]
Water	3.[illegible]3	3.4[illegible]		3.[illegible]7 %
Lead	[illegible]0	[illegible].12		1.[illegible] %

The salt was prepared repeatedly afterwards & the analyses leave no doubt but that the composition is $KPbBr_3.H_2O$ the crystal form in every case was the same.

Similar Efforts were made to prepare the corresponding Sodium Bromo Plumbite, but all failed. It was thought at one time that the salt had been obtained as lath-shaped crystals separated from the solution of Lead Bromide in Sodium Bromide But this proved on analysis to be Lead Bromide

Efforts were also [illegible] to prepare the salt by using hot Sodium Bromide

[illegible] out [illegible] salt which separates on cooling was shown
by analysis to be Lead Bromide
Undoubtedly the salt is formed
in solution but tho yet it has
been found impossible to isolate
it.

Potassium Lead Plumbite

Similar statements are made by
Berthelot[1] in regard to this salt
as in the case of the Barium Plumbite
and equally indefinite
statements[2] [illegible]
[illegible]
[illegible] [illegible] formulas.

1 [illegible] 21 [illegible] 13
2 Jahresbericht [illegible] 2

The investigation was then turned to the preparation of this salt Potassium Chloro Plumbite.

A cold saturated solution of Potassium Chloride was heated to boiling & a solution of Lead Nitrate (cold saturated) added gradually, the mass being continuously stirred, & on cooling a salt crystallized out in long white needles which on analyses showed the following results.

Percentage of Lead

Amount of salt used [illegible] 2 [illegible]

Lead Sulphate [illegible] 1

Weight of substance [illegible] 1.2[illegible] grms

Lead Sulphate [illegible]116

Lead [illegible]

Percentage of Lead 57.73

Summary

	Found		Calculated for $KPbCl_3$
	Analysis I	Analysis II	
Lead	57.81	57.73	58.71

There is no water of crystallization in this salt.

Instead of cooling the solution rapidly as was done above, if it be cooled slowly & kept at about 30° the Potassium Chloro Plumbite can be obtained in beautiful crystals & sometimes needle shaped, [illegible] [illegible] [illegible] [illegible] [illegible] [illegible] [illegible] the above mentioned [illegible] [illegible] [illegible] [illegible] [illegible]

[illegible] in the crystal, for on heating to almost 200° the salt decrepitates just as Potassium Chloride does when heated, these salts are necessarily impure on account of the large excess of Potassium Chloride present in the solution.

In efforts to prepare the Sodium Chloro-Plumbite failed. A salt crystallizing in radiating leaflets was obtained but this on analysis was found to be Lead Chloride.

...se work on the Fluoro-Plumbites could not be carried on any further on account of the want of time, but a few qualitative experiments showed that if cold saturated solution of Lead Nitrate ~~xxxx~~ be added to a cold saturated solution of Potassium Fluoride heated almost to boiling a small portion of the Lead Fluoride so formed is dissolved. But less of the Lead salt is dissolved in this case than in ~~xxxx~~ the case of either the Iodide, Bromide, or Chloride,

. . .

It ~~was~~ hoped that the investigation could be extended to the mixed halides but want of time prevented this

. . . . .

Conclusion

The principal results of this investigation may be summed up as follows,

1st — Of the six Iodo Plumbites of Potassium described by Barclay, Ditte, and Berthelot, only one exists, that is the salt $KPbI_3, 2H_2O$

2nd The Bromo Plumbite of Potassium is a well crystallized compound having the composition $KPbBr_3, H_2O$

3rd The Chloro Plumbite of Potassium can also be prepared in well formed crystals & has the composition $KPbCl_3$.

" the quantity of the Lead Halide dissolved in the alkaline halide increases with the atomic weight of the Halogen, thus only a small quantity of Lead Fluoride dissolves in a solution Potassium Fluoride, a larger quantity of Lead Chloride in Potassium Chloride solution, a still larger quantity of ~~Potassium~~ Lead Bromide in Potassium Bromide & greatest of all Lead Iodide in Potassium Iodide solution,

—

" ... Sodium salts are, if formed, separated with great difficulty ... in the case of the Sodio Plumbite while ...

isolated in the case of the Sodium Bromo or Chloro Plumbite.

— — — —

6. That all of these salts are decomposed by water, & in order for these salts to exist in solution a certain minimum amount of alkali hydride must be present this amount varying inversely as the atomic weight of the halogen atom present in the compound.

— — —

7. That the water of crystallization decreases as the atomic weight of the halogen decreases, thus

~~K PbI3 — K Br~~

$NaPbI_3 . 2H_2O$ — $KPbBr_3 . H_2O$ — $KPbCl_3$

8° ... in this sense but as comparison of all these salts allows them to be expressed by formulas in which two halogen atoms play the part of a linking oxygen atom, thus proving these salts to be no exception to the law of combination of alkali haloides with other haloides put forward by Professor Remsen & mentioned in the Introduction to this investigation.

These salts are to be represented thus;

$KPbI_3 . 2H_2O$ or $Pb<^{I}_{(I_2)}K . 2H_2O$

$KPbBr_3 . H_2O$ or $Pb<^{Br}_{(Br_2)}K . H_2O$

$KPbCl_3$ or $Pb<^{Cl}_{(Cl_2)}K .$

A possible explanation of the results obtained by Barclay, Ditte & Berthelot is this: In preparing the Iodo Plumbites two salts are used, Lead Iodide and Potassium Iodide, neither of which contains any water of crystallization. Now the Iodo-plumbite of Potassium contains two molecules of water of crystallization & if the solutions are concentrated then in the formation of the Iodo Plumbite a large amount of this water is taken up as water of crystallization by the Iodo Plumbite. This means to concentrate the solution very much & cause the ions

separation of potassium iodide which is present in large quantities occurs.
This cannot cause the analyses of the salts to show a much larger proportion of Potassium Iodide than actually belongs to the true compound.

Three other exceptions to the Law of combination in [illegible] double halides have been found viz $SnCl_2 . 2KCl . 3H_2O$ described by Poggiale; $SbCl_3$ CsCl described by Godeffroy and $CuCl . 2KCl$, discovered by Mitscherlich. [illegible] regarded to be salt $SnCl_2$ [illegible] Mr. G. M. Richardson working in this Laboratory has shown

by showing that his salt does not exist, and similarly, Mr. C. E. Saunders also working in this Laboratory, has shown that the salt $SbCl_3 \cdot nCsCl$ does not exist.

Finally in regard to the salt CuCl.2KCl the evidence points at present to the correctness of this formula, but more work is still needed on this compound. [x]

This last salt therefore is the only real exception to the law as first formed by Professor Remsen.

Biographical.

The author of this dissertation Chas. H. Herty, son of B. R. Herty, was born on the fourth day of December 1867 in Milledgeville Ga. In 1879 he entered the Middle Georgia Military and Agricultural College at Milledgeville Ga, this being a branch of the State University, where he spent five years graduating on July 2, 1884. In October of this year he entered the Junior Class of the State University at Athens Ga, graduating with the degree of Ph. B on July 12, 1886. In the following October he entered Johns Hopkins University where he has pursued the studies of Chemistry, Mineralogy and Geology.

www.ingramcontent.com/pod-product-compliance
Lightning Source LLC
Chambersburg PA
CBHW020609030726
47497CB00007B/2154

* 9 7 8 3 3 3 7 3 8 0 3 1 1 *